D0194306

Don't Go In The Cellar

by

Jeremy Strong

Illustrated by Scoular Anderson

You do not need to read this page – just get on with the book!

First published in 2003 in Great Britain by
Barrington Stoke Ltd, Sandeman House, Trunk's Close,
55 High Street, Edinburgh EH1 1SR
www.barringtonstoke.co.uk

Reprinted 2005

ISBN 1-842991-27-2

Printed in Great Britain by Bell & Bain Ltd

Meet The Author – Jeremy Strong

What is your favourite animal?
A cat
What is your favourite boy's name?
Magnus Pinchbottom
What is your favourite girl's name?
Wobbly Wendy
What is your favourite food?
Chicken Kiev (I love garlic)
What is your favourite music?
Soft
What is your favourite hobby?
Sleeping

Meet The Illustrator – Scoular Anderson

What is your favourite animal?
Humorous dogs
What is your favourite boy's name?
Orlando
What is your favourite girl's name?
Esmerelda
What is your favourite food?
Garlicky, tomatoey pasta
What is your favourite music?
Big orchestras
What is your favourite hobby?
Long walks

Discover more about Jeremy Strong and his books ... visit his website:
www.jeremystrong.co.uk

Contents

Chapter 1
The Writing on the Wall

"Why does Laura have to come and stay?" asked Zack.

"Because her mum's my best friend and I want to help her out. She has to go away for a few days," explained Zack's mum, Mrs Dawson.

"But I don't like Laura."

"You don't have to like her, she's almost family."

Zack went up to his bedroom, sat on the bed and stared at the wall. Laura was coming to stay. There was no escape. Zack did not like Laura. There were several reasons for this.

1. She was a girl.

2. She was clever.

3. She had pushed him into the paddling pool. (OK, he was only four at the time, but he still remembered. It had been wet. Very wet. And Laura had laughed. A lot.)

4. Laura had pushed Zack into the paddling pool, so Zack pushed her into the flowerbed. Then Zack had laughed a lot, but not for long. Most of Mum's best flowers had been broken when Laura had fallen on them.

It was all Zack's fault and his mum had told him off. Zack thought this was most unfair since Laura had started it. This was the first time Zack had seen how painful and difficult life could be.

Now they were both twelve and Zack still didn't like Laura. He remembered her as a short girl with a fat round face and spiky black hair. He sat on his bed and sulked.

To make matters worse, Zack's family had only just moved into their new house. It was a long way from where they lived before, and Zack was feeling pretty stressed about the whole thing. He had a new house to get used to, a new street and new faces next door. Then there was the new school, new teachers, new town, new shops and so on and so on.

Do not go in the cellar.

Zack's father, Mr Dawson, had changed jobs and that was why they had moved such a long way. They had only been in the new house for three days and already the place was going to be invaded by a stranger – the Bogey from the Paddling Pool – Laura.

Zack sighed. He lay down on his side and stared moodily at the wall. It was a bright day outside and the sun poured into the bedroom, picking out every detail in the room. Maybe that was why Zack noticed the writing. He would not have been able to see it at night, or even in dim light. Now it was quite clear.

There was writing on the bedroom wall, low down, right in front of where Zack was staring. The letters were very small and written in what looked like felt tip. This is what they said:

Do not go in the cellar

Just that, nothing else.

Do not go in the cellar

Zack propped himself up on one elbow and thought. He had seen this message before. When they had arrived at the new house there had been an old wardrobe left behind in his bedroom. Zack had looked inside. It was quite empty, but on the inside of one of the doors a message had been scratched with a sharp point.

Do not go in the cellar

The weird thing was – the new house didn't have a cellar. So what was going on?

Chapter 2
Laura

"Laura's here!" Mrs Dawson called to Zack from downstairs. He already knew. He had heard the taxi pulling away from the house. He had heard the doorbell ring and then voices from downstairs.

"Come down and say hello," Mrs Dawson called up to him. She turned to Laura and beamed a smile at her. "Zack's a bit shy," she said.

Upstairs, Zack heard his mother and turned bright red. Why did parents always get these things wrong? Why did they always embarrass him? Zack closed his eyes and counted to ten, slowly. He went downstairs.

"Hi," said Laura. "I like your new house." She smiled and her face lit up. Zack mumbled a greeting.

"My, how you've grown," said Mr Dawson, taking Laura's bag.

Zack rolled his eyes. People always said that. Why did they bother? *Of course she's grown!* he wanted to shout. That's what children do as they get older! We haven't seen her for eight years! She's bound to have grown!

But he didn't say anything. He trailed behind as Dad gave Laura a tour of the new house. While she looked at the rooms, Zack looked at her. In fact, he thought, she had grown. Zack had not been expecting her to be like this. She was almost as tall as he was. Her hair was still black but now it was so long she had to keep pushing it behind her ears to keep it out of the way. Her face was full of laughter.

Mr Dawson finished his tour of the house. "So there we are," he said. "That's Zack's room along there, and you'll be in here."

Zack had a sudden idea. "Show her the cellar, Dad," he said.

Mr Dawson shook his head. "That's the third time he's asked me, Laura. I keep telling him there isn't one. I think he's having some kind of joke with me, but I don't think it's very funny."

Laura laughed and Zack frowned.
Mr Dawson went downstairs and left them
to it.

"What's so special about the cellar?"
asked Laura.

"It's special because it doesn't exist,"
answered Zack, with what he hoped was a
smile full of dark mystery.

"Do you always talk in riddles?" asked
Laura.

Zack hesitated, wondering whether he
should show Laura the writing on the wall.

In the end he could not resist.

"Come and see," he said and they went
to his room.

He showed her the wardrobe first of all.
"This was the only piece of furniture left

behind by the last people to live here," he explained, while Laura peered at the message behind the door.

"How do you know the writing is about this house?" asked Laura. "It might have been written in another house and then the wardrobe was moved here."

"I had managed to work that out for myself," grunted Zack. He pointed to his bed. "You lie down there," he said.

Laura giggled. "Do you fancy me, then?"

Zack had no idea that he could turn as red as he did then. In fact he might just as well have stood there with a label on his chest saying TOMATO KETCHUP. He almost shouted at her.

"No I don't! I want you to read something. You can only read it if you are lying there with your face to the wall."

Laura smiled and did as she was told. Zack moved his bedside light so that it shone on the tiny words.

"Do not go in the cellar," read Laura. She sat up and looked at Zack. "Well," she began, "if this house does have a cellar, my guess is that it's downstairs somewhere. How exciting! It's just like Harry Potter. Come on!"

Zack trailed slowly after her. Somehow he felt his life was being taken over.

Chapter 3

The Cellar

Zack and Laura spent hours looking for the cellar. Mrs Dawson was surprised at how well the two of them seemed to be getting on.

"I think Zack's taken a shine to Laura," she told Mr Dawson.

"How can you tell? He just seems to snap at her all the time."

"That's what I mean," Mum explained. "Of course, Zack doesn't realise he's taken a shine to her."

Her husband looked at her for several seconds and shook his head. "Women are very strange creatures," he said. He watched Zack and Laura walk past the window. "So if Zack's taken a shine to her, has she taken a shine to him?"

"Oh heavens! Laura's liked Zack since she was four! That's why she pushed him into the paddling pool!" exclaimed Mrs Dawson.

Mr Dawson shook his head again. "I shall never understand women," he muttered.

Luckily, Laura and Zack had no idea that Zack's parents were talking in this way about them. They were far too busy looking for the cellar. They had covered every square metre of the house from the inside, and had found nothing.

Zack had even tapped the walls and the floor, hoping to sound out any hollow spaces where an opening to a cellar may be hidden. But there was nothing.

They went into the garden and tried to find an entrance from outside the house.

"It could be anywhere," sighed Zack.

"Not anywhere," said Laura smugly. "It couldn't be in China, for example. It's got to be near the house. In fact it's probably right up against the house wall. What about the greenhouse?"

"It's full of junk," said Zack.

"I know. Come on." Laura pushed her way into the greenhouse. It was very small and most of the space was taken up with old planks and piles of pots and shelving and general rubbish.

"This is more of a dump than a greenhouse," muttered Zack.

Laura looked hard at where the greenhouse joined on to one wall of the house. It was covered with a pile of old shelves.

"Help me move this lot. It might be behind here." They struggled with the big planks. Everything had to be shuffled around the greenhouse so that they could move the shelving.

"Well, well, well," murmured Zack. They had uncovered an old door. In fact, it was more like half a door. It started at ground level but only came up as far as their chests. However, it *was* a door. Someone had used red paint to leave a message on it. This time the lettering was a lot more bold.

Do not go in the cellar

"I think we'd better go in," grinned
Laura.

"Do you always do what you're told not to do?" asked Zack.

"Of course," she replied. She turned the handle, leaned against the door and gave a great shove. She almost fell inside and Zack had to grab her to stop her falling down a dark flight of steps. He pulled her back and she stumbled against him.

Laura fluttered her eyelashes at him. "You're so strong," she smiled sweetly.

"Oh shut up," muttered Zack, and led the way down.

The smell was stale and metallic. It was not nasty, just different. They found themselves in a small room. A gigantic machine filled all the space. It was covered with dust and cobwebs. The machine had enormous wheels with hundreds of cogs to make them go round. Huge metal rods and giant chains linked the wheels and there were pulleys and levers for lifting things and pistons to move up and down.

At the far end of the room was a big metal chest. What could be inside? On one side was a large lever. On top of the chest was a dirty glass window, the size and shape of a letterbox. Zack used his sleeve to rub the window clean. He looked inside but he couldn't see anything.

"I don't know what that window is for," he said.

"How about this?" asked Laura, with her hand on the lever. "What does this do?"

"I don't think we should touch it," said Zack.

So Laura pulled the lever. She *had* warned him. She always did what she was told not to. The machinery began to grind

and creak and roar. The wheels turned. The chains creaked. Pistons pounded backwards and forwards. The floor began to shake. There was a noisy *clunk* and a word appeared in the dirty window slot. Zack peered down. It said:

HORROR

"What does that mean?" asked Laura cheerfully.

A moment later she found out.

A skeleton jumped on her back.

Chapter 4

Horror

"Aaargh! Aaargh! Get it off me!" shrieked Laura.

Zack grabbed a broom. He battered at the clacking bones until they fell in a heap around Laura's feet. She stared down at the pile of bones in horror. Then, all at once, they got themselves back together and went skittering off. Laura's face was drained of blood.

"What's going on?" she whispered,
looking round in terror. But the cellar was
silent and still. Two eyes glowed in the
gloom. Then four eyes, six eyes, a hundred
eyes. Laura clung to Zack. Zack clung to
Laura. "We're being watched," she
whispered. "Who are they? What do they
want?"

"Move towards the stairs, very slowly,"
Zack said quietly.

Voices began to whisper in the dark. There seemed to be dozens of them, chattering and smacking their lips. "Zack? Laura? Come over here. We want to eat you. Oh yummy yum! Oh yes! An arm for me and a leg for you! Yum yum yum!"

Laura and Zack reached the bottom of the stairs.

"Run for it!" yelled Zack, pushing Laura in front of him. They scrambled up the steps and almost fell into the daylight. Sunshine at last! Zack looked around. It was all right. Everything was back to normal. No skeletons. No monsters. They were safe. Zack wondered if Laura could hear his heart thumping.

"You're a mess," he told her, brushing a mass of cobwebs from her hair.

She gazed back at him with big, wide eyes. They were like dark whirlpools, sucking him in.

"You saved my life," she murmured.

Zack couldn't answer. He was gobsmacked.

A distant voice called from inside, breaking the spell. "Zack? Laura? It's lunchtime. Come on!"

Mrs Dawson's voice sounded so calm, so normal. It was what they both needed to hear. They just wanted to forget what had happened.

"Come on, lunch is almost on the table," called Mrs Dawson from the kitchen.

"Don't say a word," Zack murmured to Laura as they went in.

"They wouldn't believe us anyway," she whispered back.

Zack sat at the table in a daze. He'd saved her life? Had he, really? He wasn't so sure. He didn't feel as if he'd saved her life. He felt muddled – very muddled.

"So, how are you two getting on after all these years?" asked Mr Dawson. Zack gave a shrug. Mr Dawson gave his wife a broad wink. Zack saw, and sank into an angry silence.

"I've made a pie," said Mrs Dawson. She pulled open the oven door, reached in and screamed. She screamed and screamed and screamed.

It was not a pie that was coming out of the oven. It was a giant, hairy spider, as big as an octopus. It had legs like giant chopsticks, clicking and clacking in their

search for food. It had enormous jaws. It had eight huge, bulging eyes. One eye looked at Zack. One eye looked at Laura. One eye looked at Mrs Dawson and the other five stared at Mr Dawson.

Mr Dawson leaped forward and slammed the oven door, almost squashing the spider. He turned up the heat. From inside the oven there came a weird howling and a strong smell of sizzling hair.

Mrs Dawson was trembling all over, pointing at the oven. She couldn't speak. Her hair stood on end. Beneath the tablecloth, Laura was gripping Zack's hand.

Zack gulped hard. "So, no pie then," he said, forcing a smile. "What's for pudding?"

Laura gazed carefully round the room. First a skeleton, then a giant spider. What on earth was going to happen next? "The walls!" she gasped. "Look at the walls!"

The kitchen walls appeared to be coming alive. They were heaving and juddering, as if something was about to burst through. Little holes appeared, like little dots, rapidly getting bigger and bigger. And out of the holes came ...

Giant slugs – slugs as big as a man's arm.

Mr Dawson ran to Mrs Dawson and threw his arms round her. "What do we do?" they yelled.

"Quick!" cried Laura. She pulled at Zack and dragged him outside. "We must get back in the cellar and change the machine!"

Chapter 5

The Story Machine

They almost fell down the stairs, knocking another rattling skeleton flying as they tumbled into the cellar.

"Quick!" panted Laura. "Help me push the lever back to where it was!"

They grabbed the rusty pole and pushed with all their might, but there was no way it was going to go back.

"It won't work," cried Laura, in despair.

"We can't just give up," insisted Zack. "My mum and dad are being attacked by giant slugs. Come on – let's see if it will move the other way."

Together they heaved and pushed at the lever once more. Slowly, millimetre by tiny millimetre, it began to budge. There was a great crash and the lever almost flung itself forward. *CLUNK!*

A new label flashed up into the little window. Laura and Zack peered at it.

FAIRY TALE

Laura wrinkled her nose and glanced at Zack. "Fairy Tale?" she asked. Zack took a quick look around the cellar. No skeletons. Phew! Things seemed to have gone back to normal, if only for a minute or two.

"I think I know what all this is," Zack began slowly, patting the top of the chest. "I reckon this is like some kind of story machine. It makes different kinds of stories. The first kind was horror, and now it's ..."

"... going to make a fairy tale," nodded Laura, her eyes wide. "That will be why there's a dragon behind you."

Zack whirled round, only to see something very small scuttle behind the old table. Zack smiled and relaxed. It was a dragon all right, but it was only the size of a small shoebox. Poor thing! It must be scared of them. Zack made quiet, clucking noises and slowly reached out a hand to pick up the little creature.

Laura watched, holding her breath. *How could Zack pick the dragon up? Suppose it tried to bite him? Suppose it could breathe*

fire? All at once her heart almost stopped dead. *SUPPOSE THE BABY DRAGON'S MOTHER WAS JUST AROUND THE CORNER?*

Even as this thought entered her head there was a loud crashing and bashing. Bricks burst from the wall and a knight in shining silver armour came crashing through. He was waving a great two-handed sword, and the broad, blue blade shone and sparkled as he swung it round and round.

"All right, where's the dragon?" he boomed angrily. "I know there's a dragon in here. I am Sir Knight-in-Shining-Armour and my sword, Dragon-Slicer, always glows blue like this when there's a dragon nearby. I must slay it at once."

"But it's just a baby," protested Zack, holding the little creature even closer. The knight strode towards him. Zack felt the wind as the sword sliced the air above his head.

"Babies grow up!" roared Sir Knight. "I am the dragon slayer! Hand it over at once!" He stepped forward again, raising his sword high above his head. Zack cowered before him, certain that he was going to die, along with the baby dragon.

Laura's brain was bursting with the effort of trying to think. What could she do? Her face suddenly lit up. Yes! It might work! She hurried to the bottom of the steps and began to wail and moan and pull at her hair in despair.

The knight turned towards her at once. "What? A damsel in distress? I must save her at once." He moved across to Laura, going down on one knee before her. "Fair maiden," he began, much to Laura's surprise. After all, her hair was black, but she let him go on. "What is the matter?

Are you about to be eaten by wolves? Is a wicked wizard about to turn you into a caterpillar? How can I help you?"

"Oh woe and misery," moaned Laura, still pretending to be a poor princess. She held the back of one hand to her forehead and let out a terrible groan. "There are giant slugs in the kitchen and they are about to eat my friend's parents! Nobody but you can save them!"

Zack was pretty amazed at this. *Hmmm,* he thought, *she's pretty cunning. She's saving me and my parents all in one go. That's a neat trick!*

"Do not fear!" cried Sir Knight-in-Shining-Armour. "I shall slay those slimy slugs and we shall all live happily ever after!"

"My hero!" sighed Laura, and she fluttered her eyelashes at the knight.

Zack frowned. Only half an hour earlier Laura had been fluttering her eyelashes at him.

Sir Knight-in-Shining-Armour went charging up the stairs and Zack and Laura followed. Outside they met with yet another strange sight.

A crowd of people were pressing round Zack's house, and they seemed to be eating it.

Chapter 6

The Pie Arrives at Last

"Hmmm, lovely gingerbread," mumbled one man, chewing on a mouthful of window frame.

It was only too true. The house walls were made of gingerbread. The roof was cake icing. The window ledges were made of chocolate. No wonder people were eating the house.

There was no sign of the giant slugs. In fact Zack's parents were now marching crossly up and down, trying to pull the crowd of munchers off the sides of the house.

"Do you mind?" they were saying. "This is our house! Kindly stop eating my front door! And you – look what you've done. You've left teeth marks all over the doorstep."

There was a loud crumbling noise and the garage suddenly collapsed. All of one wall had been eaten away by the crowd, leaving the garage with nothing to hold it up.

"They're eating us out of house and home," cried Mrs Dawson. "I don't understand it. First we had a giant spider, then slugs and now our house is being eaten before our very eyes. And why is there a knight in shining armour clanking about the place? Oh, it's all too much."

Zack and Laura looked at each other and nodded. "Back to the cellar, I suppose," muttered Zack. "How long is this going to go on for, do you think?"

Laura shrugged. "I haven't a clue. Come on, we'd better hurry, or there'll be nothing left of your house."

Back in the cellar they pushed at the lever once more. *CLUNK!*

"What does it say?" Zack asked in a nervous voice.

"SLAPSTICK," Laura read out. "What do you think that means? Urffff!"

A large custard pie suddenly arrived from nowhere and landed slap bang in her face. She wiped the custard away from her eyes and glared at Zack.

"Did you do that, Zack? I'll get you!" Laura dived forwards, slipped on a large banana skin and fell flat on her face.

Zack was laughing his head off.

"It's like the circus, Laura!" he shouted. "It's really funny."

This made Laura even crosser.

She struggled to her feet and set off after him once again. Zack turned to run, but his trousers caught on a sharp hook. There was an awful tearing noise and a large flap of torn cloth hung down from his bottom.

"Oh no!"

It was Laura's turn to laugh. "I can see your pants!" she cried, dancing round and round in delight. "I can see your pants!"

Now Zack was chasing Laura. She fled up the stairs and out into the garden, where a pie war seemed to have broken out. Pies of every sort and size were flying all over the place. An apple pie landed splat on Zack's chest. A small cream tart got him bang on

his right ear. Someone squeezed a large
tube and a jet of tomato paste shot across
the garden and got Mr Dawson on the head.

Mrs Dawson was stumbling round with
one foot stuck in a bucket. Laura was
suddenly drenched with the hose that Zack
aimed at her. He didn't even know they had
a hose. It just seemed to appear in his hand.

He dropped it in surprise. This was so
weird!

And then Zack saw what was happening
to the house. It was no longer made of
gingerbread. It was a real house once again,
but – and it was a very big BUT – one whole
side of the house was falling over.

An entire wall was falling towards them.
It was going to crush them. "Look out!"
yelled Zack. "Look out!"

They all stopped and stared, frozen to
the spot, as the great wall came rushing
towards them, rushing, rushing, until ...

CRASH!

Zack screwed his eyes up tight. The wall
hit the ground with a shuddering thud. Zack
couldn't believe it. He was still standing.
He was still alive. He opened his eyes and
looked around. They were all still standing.

By some amazing stroke of luck each one of them had been standing where an open window frame had landed. They stood there, in the window frames, with the house wall lying all around them. They looked at each other in total amazement.

"Wow," murmured Laura, with a little smile. "That was lucky!"

"You've got custard in your hair," Zack told her.

"Pants!" Laura snapped back, and Zack, without thinking, put both hands on his bottom.

Chapter 7

Buckets of Blood

"Can someone please explain what is going on?" asked Mr Dawson. "It's like some strange dream."

"More like a nightmare," said Mrs Dawson.

"It's the cellar," Zack began.

"There isn't a cellar!" cried his father. "Stop going on about it."

"There *is* a cellar," said Laura. "We've been inside it. There's a machine down there making all these things happen, and we can't get it to stop. Everything has to be slapstick at the moment, and that will go on until we change it."

"What comes after slapstick?" asked Mrs Dawson.

"That's just the problem," Zack explained. "We don't know until we push the lever."

By this time all four of them were down in the cellar. They were struggling to reach the machine. They had to battle through the huge piles of banana skins, whizzing pies and squirting hoses. On top of that their trousers kept falling down, no matter what they did.

They all heaved on the lever. *CLUNK!*

MURDER MYSTERY

"Oh dear," sighed Mrs Dawson. "I don't like the sound of that."

Almost as if someone had been listening, there was a chilling scream and a dead body landed on the table right beside Mrs Dawson. There was an awful thud as the body hit the table and a shower of blood slopped across her.

The dead man had an axe stuck in his head, an arrow through his heart, a dagger in his stomach and a rope around his neck.

"Aha!" cried a stern voice from the far corner of the cellar. "Caught in the act! I am the Great Detective and I arrest you, Mrs Karen Dawson, for the murder of Lord Plummy-Wotsit."

"But I didn't do it!" declared Mrs Dawson.

"Then why are your hands covered in blood? It's a perfect match, too. Look – his blood is red and the blood on your hands is red. Aha!"

"All blood is red," Zack pointed out.

"And I arrest you for assisting your mother in the murder of Lord Plummy-Wotsit," cried the Great Detective.

"But sir, they couldn't have done it,"
Laura told him. "They were both with me."

The Great Detective took a step back.
"They were with you? Aha! Can you prove
it?"

"Of course I can, because I was with ...
him!" Laura pointed at Mr Dawson in a
dramatic way. The Great Detective

frowned. "And you, sir," he demanded. "Where were you?"

"I was with you," replied Mr Dawson, pointing at the Great Detective.

"Aha! ... I mean, what? Really? With me?" The Great Detective began with a splutter. "But, but, but that means *I DID IT!* I am the murderer!"

The body on the table sat up, dripping blood in every direction, and Lord Plummy-Wotsit gave a great sigh.

"The whole lot of you are perfectly useless," complained Lord Plummy-Wotsit. "None of you did it. The butler stabbed me. The maid strangled me. The gardener shot me with his bow and arrow and then I stuck an axe in my head."

Lord Plummy-Wotsit got off the table and squelched across the cellar. "I'm fed up with all this murder anyhow. Look what it's done to my suit. Blood everywhere! Well it's jolly well going to stop." He reached out and pulled the lever. *CLUNK!*

Everyone else crowded round the little window and stared at the next word.

Chapter 8
Don't Look!

ROMANCE

That was what it said. Romance.

Zack peered carefully round the room.
His mum and dad had gone. He was alone
with Laura. The cellar was filled with
sunlight. A bluebird twittered in one
corner. Several butterflies fluttered past.
The sweet smell of roses filled the air.
Somewhere they could hear a waterfall

doing what waterfalls do – splishy-
splashing.

Laura smiled at Zack. She fluttered her
eyelashes. "You're so brave," she murmured.
"And good looking."

Zack gulped. He wanted to say: *Don't
come any closer!* He wanted to say: *What's
happening to me?* He wanted to yell: *HELP!*
But he couldn't. He simply could not do it.
Instead, his mouth opened, his lips moved,
and he heard himself say, "I think you are
the most beautiful girl I have ever seen."

This was an interesting thing for Zack
to say, because by this time Laura looked a
bit of a mess. She was still covered with the
remains of pies and tarts, as well as a large
quantity of Lord Plummy-Wotsit's blood.
Her face and hair were streaked with dirt.
Despite all this, Zack thought Laura looked
beautiful, and he told her so.

"You haven't always liked me, have you?" asked Laura, taking a step closer to Zack.

He shook his head. "You pushed me in the paddling pool," he reminded her.

"And you pushed me into your mum's flowerbed," she reminded him.

"You pushed me first," Zack insisted.

"I only pushed you because I liked you," said Laura. "I've always liked you," she added, taking another step closer.

Zack felt as if his feet were rooted to the spot. He wasn't sure now if he wanted to run away or wait and see what would happen next. Laura was much nearer. He could hear her breathing. He could feel her warmth. She reached out to him. She raised her face to his. She pressed against him and he leaned back. *CLUNK!*

He had pushed against the lever. Zack came to as if he'd been woken from a deep dream. He hurled himself away from Laura. He couldn't believe it! They had been about to kiss! Him and Laura!

Laura was gazing at the glass. "It's empty," she sighed. "It doesn't say anything. It's over."

"Thank heavens for that," muttered Zack. "Come on. We have work to do."

He grabbed Laura by the hand and pulled her up the stairs and out of the cellar. Together they pushed the cellar door shut. Zack nailed a big piece of wood across it. He found an old paintbrush and half a tin of paint. He set to work with the brush and added two words to the warning on the cellar door, one at the beginning and one at the end.

DEFINITELY

Do not go in the cellar

EVER

"That should do it," he said.

The two of them went out to the garden and threw themselves down on the grass. They were worn out by everything that had happened. Zack lay there and felt the warm sunshine on his face. He turned towards Laura. Her face was turned towards him, but her eyes were closed. Zack wondered if she had fallen asleep.

Oh well, he thought, *she was, well, OK for a girl. In fact she was ...*

Laura's eyes opened and he found her gazing at him.

"We've had a lucky escape," he said gruffly. "Who knows what might have happened?"

"Who knows what will happen?" suggested Laura, and her fingers touched his arm. "Who knows?"

Barrington Stoke was a famous and much-loved story-teller. He travelled from village to village carrying a lantern to light his way. He arrived as it grew dark and when the young boys and girls of the village saw the glow of his lantern, they hurried to the central meeting place. They were full of excitement and expectation, for his stories were always wonderful.

Then Barrington Stoke set down his lantern. In the flickering light the listeners were enthralled by his tales of adventure, horror and mystery. He knew exactly what they liked best and he loved telling a good story. And another. And then another. When the lantern burned low and dawn was nearly breaking, he slipped away. He was gone by morning, only to appear the next day in some other village to tell the next story.

Barrington Stoke would like to thank all its readers for commenting on the manuscript before publication and in particular:

Alex Ballard	Jane Hodges	Alex Pike
Jamie Beattie	Giles Holley	Edward Potter
Hilda Biagi	Sarah Hosie	Lucy Robinson
Harriet Cornock	Jamie Hughes	Danny Scott
Phoebe Cox	Jennifer Hunter	Zak Shotton
Phillip Critoph	Edgar Johnson	Christian Sitch
Pippa Cusack	Mohammed Kadiri	Jay Tamer
Scott Edwards	Marie Leahy	Mrs P.M. Taylor
Youssfe Elidrissi	Joe MacDonald	Bethan Thomas
Daisy Elt	Mary McGovern	Tim Whishaw
Euan Findlay	Gavin McLean Paris	Willis-Hughes
Lucien Fraser	Kerri Milne	Edward Wood
Jan Gibbons	Harry Milne	Marc Wood
Mairi Hodge	Mobarik Omer	

Become a Consultant!

Would you like to give us feedback on our titles before they are published? Contact us at the email address or website below – we'd love to hear from you!

E-mail: info@barringtonstoke.co.uk
Website: www.barringtonstoke.co.uk